T0082773

THE LIFE
AND LEGEND
OF THE
COCO BED KID

THE LIFE
AND LEGEND
OF THE
COCO BED KID

HARVIS (JUNIOR) JOHNSON

THE LIFE AND LEGEND OF THE COCO BED KID

iUniverse books may be ordered through booksellers or by contacting:

iUniverse
1663 Liberty Drive
Bloomington, IN 47403
www.iuniverse.com
844-349-9409

Because of the dynamic nature of the Internet, any web addresses or links contained in this book may have changed since publication and may no longer be valid. The views expressed in this work are solely those of the author and do not necessarily reflect the views of the publisher, and the publisher hereby disclaims any responsibility for them.

Any people depicted in stock imagery provided by Getty Images are models, and such images are being used for illustrative purposes only.
Certain stock imagery © Getty Images.

ISBN: 978-1-6632-0871-2 (sc)
ISBN: 978-1-6632-0872-9 (e)

Print information available on the last page.

iUniverse rev. date: 10/13/2020

Note of Appreciation

I would like to sincerely thank my Editors and all the Staff at iUniverse for their patience and professional assistance in helping put my thoughts into this Book. My old friend James with the Ink Spot in Natchitoches, La. who kindly worked with me in putting my manuscript together, as well as his assistance with the cover photo.

As with my precious two Books, I sincerely appreciate the talented work by my lifelong friend David Carr, who created the sketches that introduced each Chapter. My wonderful Grandson Noah Harvis for his constant encouragement. He has been by my side throughout this process, as he has been for the past year as I am currently battling Bone Marrow Leukemia.

I would also like to thank my dear friend Rhonda Sanders, who affectionately dubbed me "The CoCo Bed Kid".

Finally, I want to thank those of you who spent your hard earned dollars to purchase my Book. I Pray that you will be satisfied with my story.

DEDICATION

I would like to dedicate this Book to my precious Grandson Noah Harvis Johnson. Last year when I first had thoughts of this Book begin to formulate in my mind, I was diagnosed with Bone Marrow Leukemia. My health began to deteriorate rapidly.

Noah J had been working as a Hospitality Host at Yellowstone National Park. He worked there the two previous seasons and was preparing for another tour of duty when he found out about my health.

Without any hesitation, Noah J asked me, his Papa J, as he affectionately calls me, if he could possibly pass up this upcoming season and remain to take care of me. He indicated that since he had been a reliable employee, it would be no problem if he gave them proper notice, and that he could return the following season if he chose to.

Noah J literally took over my life, which was basically nonexistent due to my health. Many times he would have to assist me in the most basic daily activities. He was there to take me to Doctor appointments, as well as to Chemotherapy Treatments. Noah J also kept our house in a clean and orderly fashion, and cooked some of the most delicious meals that I had ever eaten, when my health permitted it.

I am now in remission and Noah J has found a good job locally since he does not have to be with me all the time.

I lost my Son Kevin, Noah J's Dad, when he was a youngster. Having Noah J around is like reliving the days when his Dad was a youngster as well.

Papa J is extremely proud of his Noah J, and all that he has done for me, as well as the encouraging words he gave as I was putting this Book together.

Papa J dedicates this Book to you Noah J. I am extremely proud of you.

CHAPTER 1

That a young boy known as The CoCo Bed Kid ever existed is a fact. His name is about all anybody could ever agree on. It was not a name that he sought for himself, but one given to him from later in his life by members of the small Village of Cloutierville late in the final years of his young life.

No one can say for certainly when he began his life on the dark side of the law; however, he was very successful, and at times was called the Robin Hood of his day.

Lawmen, especially the bad ones, feared him, and vowed that if given the opportunity he would never stand trial if apprehended.

The CoCo Bed Kid had a kind heart but was quick to right a wrong when he found it. He rarely kept much of the money that he stole from Banks and greedy businessmen that he encountered. Many times a struggling farmer would find a bag of money on his doorstep as he began yet another day of struggle to support his poor family. The only thing in the bag of money was a perfectly written note with the words "Pay It Forward", The CoCo Bed Kid.

CHAPTER 2

After the Kid had left his package of money at the Johnson's home, he road silently up the dirt road on the bank of Cane River in the early dawn morning on his beautiful mare Dolly. As he slowly road by a row of shotgun dwellers he waves at some of the old black men sitting on the gallery in thread bare clothes, their jawbones protruding from lack of food, their eyes silently staring out in the distance, as if wondering how he would be able to support his starving family.

The Kid was confident that Mr. Johnson would "Pay It Forward" to these poor people with the money he had left behind. That's the way it was on this God forsaken farm that was operated by people who cared little about the misfortunes their share croppers had to endure.

Only months before, as the cotton plants began to break the rich red soil, the property owners were beginning a new experiment. This basically killed the share croppers opportunity to make a meager wage by chopping the grass from around the cotton plant.

Geese had been shipped in by the hundreds and would walk up and down the rows of cotton plants and eat the tender grass that had sprang forth. This had been the responsibility of the share croppers, to hoe around the cotton plant and remove the grass. They were affectionately known hoe hands. The owners could save money on labor since there was no cost in feeding the geese.

Had it not been for the fact that these share croppers would now had virtually no income until the cotton was ready to be picked and brought to the gin for processing, the scene was a sight to see every morning as the geese would leave their roost and began a march to the cotton fields to get their daily fill of tender grass that had sprouted up during the night.

With a bittersweet smile on his face the CoCo Bed Kid urged Dolly into a gallop and headed toward the nearby forest of tall virgin pine trees swaying in the wind. The Kid was headed to a place called the Wolf Rock Cave that overlooked Bundick Creek, deep in the forest, to meet his old friend John Murrell and his band of outlaws who used the area as a hideout.

CHAPTER 3

Night had fallen when the CoCo Bed Kid arrived at Wolf Rock Cave. It had been a long hard ride as Dolly courageously carried her master through the tall pines. Both horse and rider were exhausted. After the Kid had taken the saddle and bridle off Dolly, he led her down the hill to a little stream for a cool drink from the creek running down from a rock opening on the hillside. He then gave Dolly an ample supply of oats from his provisions and gave her a good rub down.

Exhausted, the Kid passed on supper and immediately fell asleep on his bedroll as his head rested on the saddle. As he slept, dreams from childhood filled his mind. He was brought back to a time when he was a little boy riding his favorite stick horse around his loving Parents share croppers home. When he was not riding his stick horse he was on his hands and knees pushing around a piece of wood pretending he was pulling a wagon of logs that his Dad worked in the woods to cut.

Just after dawn, after a peaceful night's sleep, the Kid walked Dolly down to the stream for water and then gave her a ration of oats. He then gathered firewood and began a fire. While his coffee pot was brewing, he then carefully opened a sack with several of the large goose eggs that he had gathered before leaving Cane River. One egg was enough to make a meal, and as the bacon fried he cracked open an egg and added it with the frying bacon in the skillet.

As the Kid was watching the bacon and egg fry he poured himself a cup of black coffee. Just as he sat back to enjoy his coffee and watch his breakfast cook, he felt the cold barrel of a gun press against the back of his head, and then the click of the hammer as it was pulled back. The Kid could not believe his misfortune. As the gun barrel pushed harder into the back of his head, the Kid began to rise and turn around. He looked into the eyes of his old friend John Murrell who broke into a hearty laugh, uncocked and holstered his pistol as he gave his old friend a huge bear hug.

CHAPTER 4

The CoCo Bed Kid was relieved to see his old friend John Murrell and his three gang members Dennis, Jerry, and Yonie. Murrell had hand picked these three men for their loyalty, fierceness, and daring. These men, along with their leader were not to be reckoned with if you cared about your safety and life.

After a lot of laughter and hugs, the Kid invited them all to join him in breakfast. All were amazed with the size and tastefulness of the large goose eggs. After their tasty breakfast and relaxing smokes, the men brought the Kid up to speed on events that had taken place since they had last seen each other, which was after they had fled Mexico over the Border in El Paso, Texas. The Mexican Federal Army had chased them to the Border after a series of daring robberies in small Mexican towns. Once safely in El Paso, Murrell and his gang, along with the Kid, had done extensive partying in the many Cantinas along the Riverwalk that the city had to offer.

The CoCo Bed Kid had decided to lay low for a while near his home, the Village of Cloutierville, where he still had many friends who would provide him safety if the need arose. The Kid's parents had been savagely murdered by Union forces during the Civil War after their victory at Monette Ferry. This had been a bitter blow upon hearing the news and seeing his old home place burned to the ground.

While the Kid was making his way back to Cloutierville, Murrell and his gang, although planning a return to the safety of their hideout at Wolf Rock Cave, decided to travel up through New Mexico and Oklahoma, robbing banks and trains, to increase their growing stash of loot.

As John Murrell and his fierce gang entered Louisiana and neared the Port City of Natchitoches, they were spotted by one of the Deputies who worked for local Sheriff Vic Jones. Once Sheriff Jones was notified of the Murrell sighting, he quickly gathered a posse of his most dedicated and proven Deputies. Jones was known in Natchitoches as a fair and tough Sheriff, and he saw this as an opportunity to rid the area of the vicious Murrell gang. This was not good news for Murrell as he cautiously led his men through the thick forest pines to their hideout.

CHAPTER 5

As John Murrell related the story of their adventures, along with being spotted by the Natchitoches Deputy, everyone felt grim, knowing that when word got back to Sheriff Jones, he would be hot on their trail. The Kid and Murrell agreed that they needed to make plans to leave the area. Murrell had another revelation for the Kid.

After the Kid's departure from El Paso, and before the Murrell gang began their carnage through New Mexico and Oklahoma, they had traveled from El Paso to Galveston for a meeting with Murrell's old friend Jean Laffitte.

The notorious Pirate had set up a sanctuary in the swampy islands surrounding Barateria Bay in Louisiana near New Orleans. Laffitte had planned to retire in these surroundings, but became restless after terrorizing shipping in the Gulf of Mexico, and moved his people to another Pirate haven on Galveston Island in Texas.

John Murrell wanted to see his old friend which was the reason for traveling to Galveston. Once there it didn't take long to find the whereabouts of Laffitte's compound. The gang was treated like royalty when the Outlaws and Pirates met up. After a lot of drinks and partying, Murrell and Laffite sat down for a serious discussion. Murrell knew that his plans to steal and rob as they traveled through New Mexico and Oklahoma would not secure enough money to set him up for the rest of his life, and that of his gang. He wanted more, and hoped Laffitte could give him the information to make this happen.

Laffitte was getting old and wanted to retire, but he shared an idea with Murrell that was intriguing. Where was a recently closed Federal Mint in New Orleans that held a fortune in gold and silver coins. Laffitte still had contacts in New Orleans, which was the reason that he possessed this information. He was happy to share this with his old friend John Murrell.

As the CoCo Bed Kid listened to Murrell's story, he became excited. If they were successful, what a haul that would be. The Kid thought back to the hollow eyes of the old black men sitting on their galleries, and at that moment decided what he would do with his share of the money. The CoCo Bed Kid was all in.

CHAPTER 6

It was mid morning before John Murrell finished his story about their visit to see the Pirate Jean Laffitte. The CoCo Bed Kid sat spellbound throughout the entire story. From the description of Laffitte and the compound that he and his fellow Pirates had set up on Galveston Island, the Kid knew that he had to meet the man, and told Murrell so.

With the knowledge that Sheriff Jones would be leading a posse in search of him, Murrell suggested that they all make a return trip to Laffitte's compound and perhaps they could convince him in joining up for one last caper before he really retired, and besides, with his knowledge of the New Orleans area, Laffitte would make a valuable asset. The Kid readily approved and they began to break camp.

Murrell asked the Kid if he needed any money but was turned down. As everyone was preparing to leave, John Murrell collected all of the loot they had accumulated from their New Mexico and Oklahoma robberies and gave each of his men a sizable amount. He then told them that he had a special hiding place in the Wolf Rock Cave, and told them he would safely store the remaining money there. While Murrell was privately taking care of this matter, the Kid and Murrell's gang exchanged a few more stories of their recent exploits.

When Murrell returned from hiding the money, it was decided that they would travel to the Port town of Shreveport. From there they would take a train to

Galveston, where it was hoped they could convince Jean Laffitte to join them.

It was well into the night when they arrived in Shreveport at the train station. Since the depot was open twenty four hours a day, they arranged for tickets, including an area in the livestock car for their horses and gear. They received permission from the ticket agent to bring their horses around to the staging area to unsaddle them. The horses were given a good rubdown and ration of oats. The men then found a nice location to spread their bedrolls and settle in for a few hours of well deserved rest and sleep. They had about six hours before the train left for Galveston.

When the sun began rising in the eastern sky the men arose and found a nearby cafe for breakfast. Yonie had them all laughing when he complained about the size of the eggs. He said that only the day before their breakfast consisted of just one egg that filled the entire plate, referring to the Kid's goose egg. Their waiter was scratching his head as he left their table.

At precisely eight o'clock the men boarded the train after seeing to it that their horses were safely loaded into the livestock car along with their gear. They all then headed to the bar car for some liquid refreshments.

The trip seemed to last forever since the train made stops in almost every little town along the way. The train ride was uneventful; however, to the silent satisfaction of the outlaw clan, they knew that Sheriff Victor Jones was far behind them.

Finally, after a long day's train ride, they began to smell the salt air rolling off the Gulf of Mexico as they neared Galveston. As the train was pulling in to the station they could see the shoreline filled with the masts of ships varying in size anchored in the harbor.

The group of men headed toward the livestock car to gather their gear and horses. On the way they encounter the Train Engineer Ricky Sanders, and the CoCo Bed Kid stopped him and deposited a sizable amount of money into his hand and said that they had enjoyed their trip.

The Murrell gang and the CoCo Bed Kid then sat out toward Jean Laffitte's compound. Murrell knew that his friend would be surprised to see them again so soon, and knew for certain that Jean would love meeting the CoCo Bed Kid.

CHAPTER 7

The CoCo Bed Kid had never been to Galveston before and was amazed at the hustle and bustle of this Port City. Along with the many ships were numerous shrimp boats offloading their haul of shrimp in the many markets along the coastal wall. The smell of boiling shrimp was too much for the Kid and he convinced John Murrell to stop at one of the outdoor cafes for some delicious boiled shrimp and corn. John agreed and sent his men, Dennis, Jerry, and Yonie to the Laffitte compound and alert his friend of their impending visit. After their bellies were filled Murrell and the Kid made their way to the compound for introduction to the Pirate.

Upon arrival the old friends embraced and the CoCo Bed Kid was introduced to Laffitte. The Kid was surprised to see the advanced age of John's friend.

They soon retired to Laffitte's private quarters and Murrell began his pitch to lure the old Pirate out of retirement for one last mission that would make them rich beyond imagination.

Laffitte listened intensely and was intrigued by Murrell's idea of robbing the New Orleans Mint, that they had discussed at their last meeting months earlier. Jean then had a confession he wanted to relate to his old friend. Not only had he retired, but he had laid the groundwork for everyone in New Orleans to believe that he had died years earlier. As far as any legal authorities knew, he did not exist. His cover in Galveston had gone smoothly and nothing could be proven in a court of law that his men were criminals. This secret of his death had gone on for years.

Laffitte admitted that the reason he retired and cease from public life came during the Civil War when he learned that H.L. Hunley had designed an under water vessel that he called a submarine. His invention torpedoed and sank the Union Warship USS Houstonic. Laffitte knew that his fierce battles on the open seas with his Warship were legendary; however, a vessel below the water was something that he did not want to deal with. He did not want to get blown from the water by a vessel that he could not see.

Murrell and the Kid acknowledged his dilemma; however, this venture would far out way the risk involved, and he knew that his old friend could not pass up this challenge if they researched it properly. Finally Laffitte began to understand the opportunity this venture would present. He had relatives in New Orleans who could gather much needed information about the Mint and make arrangements to make this project successful.

Several years before, the City of New Orleans was faced with sever prostitution and gambling problems. A huge area near the French Quarter was where this illicit activity was conducted. Commonly known as the District the name was changed to Storyville after a New Orleans City Council Member. Lavish buildings were turned into successful hotels, restaurants, and yes, brothels. One of these hotels, best in the City, along with it's restaurant, was owned by Jean's relatives David and Paul Carr. They were successful businessmen and had a pulse on everything that happened in New Orleans. The Carr's had turned over most of their business dealings to a lifelong friend of theirs by the name of Janice Adkins. Janice was an extremely talented, as well as a beautiful business woman, and handled the Carr brother's business affairs very successfully, leaving them time for other illegal activities.

A sparkle began to shine in Jean Laffitte's eyes. This would work. It was time to come back from the dead for one last hurrah. The three men all embraced and laughed about their cleverness. They retired to the party where Murrell's gang and the Laffitte Pirates were having the party of a lifetime. As The CoCo Bed Kid watched with enthusiasm, Laffitte and Murrell told the men of their plans. They were going to make one last visit to New Orleans.

Laffitte instructed his ship crew to make their way to the docks and prepare to sail on the outgoing tide the next morning. New Orleans would be their destination and he advised the others to put an end to their party and rest up for the next morning's voyage.

CHAPTER 8

The following morning everyone arose early and made their way to the Galveston docks where Laffitte's ship was anchored. During the night, following instructions from their Captain, Laffitte's men filled the vessel with all needed supplies for their voyage to the Port of New Orleans. With favorable winds the ship should make their destination by nightfall.

The CoCo Bed Kid was in awe of the view as he stood with the old Captain and John Murrell at the helm of this magnificent schooner. There was a lot of activity on the deck as the crew began pulling in lines and prepared for departure. After the Kid's and Murrell's horses and gear were safely aboard, the huge ship began its slow journey out to sea. The sky was filled with hundreds of White Sea Gulls as they swooped down into the water to grab the tiny fish that were churned up by the wake of the ship.

Once clear of the harbor, Laffitte's men ran up their massive sails that would harness the wind flow which would enable the Captain or his Pilot to navigate them to their destination. Finally the largest sail was pulled up to expose the Flag of France, Laffitte's home Country. They were finally on their way to New Orleans and yet another adventure. Excitement filled the air.

After they were well out to sea and Galveston was a tiny speck on the shoreline behind them, Laffitte gave the Kid, Murrell and his his men, a tour of his big ship. It was massive and featured luxurious surroundings that kept his crew happy. The CoCo Bed Kid was intrigued by the huge cannons that lined the lower deck on both sides. They had sunk many vessels during their days of carnage and plunder. The crew went about their day's routine merrily singing old Pirate songs.

The wind was favorable and they were making good time. By mid afternoon the giant ship entered the mouth of the mighty Mississippi River that spilled into the Gulf of Mexico. About midway up the River on their voyage to New Orleans, Laffitte pointed out the remains of two Forts on opposite sides of the River, Fort Jackson and Fort Philip. They had been part of the West Gulf Blockading Squadron, which was set up to form a blockade of the Union Navy Fleet that were planning an attack on New Orleans. Unfortunately many lives were lost on both sides and the Union Navy broke the blockade and captured New Orleans.

The Laffitte Schooner finally docked at the Port of New Orleans after nightfall. The crew began securing the great ship as The CoCo Bed Kid, along with Murrell and his men, Dennis, Jerry, and Yonie, watched with amazement at the nightlife on the dock which was filled with gayety as people were greeting friends and families getting off other ships at the dock. The gas lamps twinkling along the warf and throughout the surrounding area reminded the Kid of a swarm of lightening bugs.

Not long after they had docked Laffitte sent one of his men to a favorite clothing store to purchase he and his guests some fine clothing. Murrell and his men, along with the Kid were all admiring each other in their fine clothing when Laffitte joined them on the lower deck. They almost didn't recognize their old Pirate friend as he joined them. His disguise was amazing and he was dressed like a King. They all followed him down the gang plank to a couple of waiting horse drawn carriages that would take them to the District. One would not know that the City was still recovering from the War of Northern Aggression, as the CoCo Bed Kid bitterly called it. People were milling around everywhere and the sound of Dixieland music spilled on to the streets from the many bars and from street musicians at almost every corner.

Not long after entering the District, the two carriages arrived in front of a huge white antebellum styled four story hotel called the Chalet. As they made their way to the registration desk, Laffitte spotted his cousin David Carr who was mingling with important looking guests. When David spotted Jean, his face broke into a big smile and he hurried over and they embraced affectionately. After introductions were made all around, David led them over to the registration desk and told the clerk to fix his friends up with their most luxurious rooms on the fourth floor. While this was taking place, David's brother Paul spotted them and walked over. He embraced his Cousin as well and introductions were make again.

When the rooms were secured David led his guests from the large room to the bar. As they approached the entrance, above the door in flashing lights read "Janice's Place", the name of the Carr Brother's business partner. As David was leading his guests to a group of private tables in the bar, he spotted his business partner, Janice Adkins, as she mingled with the high rollers in order to get them to her gambling tables. David waved her over.

As everyone was being seated at their tables David introduced them all to his partner. The CoCo Bed Kid observed her grace and beauty and was almost speechless when she was introduced to him. Janice had a magnetic personality and her charm oozed with her every smile. She told everyone to enjoy themselves and said that she needed to get back to her other patrons and walked away. After a few steps she turned and smiled. The CoCo Bed Kid would have sworn that she was looking at him. She then headed back to the gaming room where the wealthy clientele were pouring money into the house winnings on her slot machines, blackjack and roulette tables.

David and Paul sat with the group for a couple of drinks with their Cousin and his friends. They related several entertaining stories to the amusement of the group. Not long after, Laffitte told the Kid and Murrell that he was going to join his Cousins in their private office for preliminary discussions for the reason of their visit.

CHAPTER 9

After Laffitte was led by the Carr's to their suite of magnificent offices and were seated, he interrupted David in his pleasantries to recommend that the CoCo Bed and John Murrell should be included in this conversation because they could possibly provide excellent insight into plans going forward. David agreed and Paul went back to their table and invited the Kid and Murrell back to his office. Dennis, Jerry, and Yonie thanked Paul and asked if he could provide a porter to help them get their gear to the respective rooms.

Once settled in David's office, Paul served them all a sniffer of their own imported brandy. David then began to explain what he and Paul had found about the New Orleans Mint.

The Mint had been in operation until the Civil War and the following Reconstruction, and had only recently reopened. There was a large supply of gold coins and ingots on hand and there was plans to move about five million dollars of their inventory to the San Francisco Mint. Plans were in the works for the United States to print paper money and have gold to back it up. One could exchange the paper for gold coins at any time. To prepare for this the San Francisco Mint needed more gold. As the California gold rush was in decline, and the fact that the San Francisco Mint had to provide the Union Army with gold during the Civil War, their supply of gold was getting dangerously low. They reached out to the New Orleans Mint to help with their needs.

The Carr brothers had their hands in many enterprises throughout New Orleans. They only used the Chalet as a front. They continued to build their fortune through their import-export business which enabled them to import contraband as well as export it to European Countries as well as the United States. To make this enterprise successful, David and Paul had many trusted employees on their payroll. They were all highly paid and loyal. Two of these trusted employees worked at the New Orleans Mint. They were so deeply imbedded that even the most secret dealings were no secret to them.

David explained this to the Kid and Murrell and brought them up to speed on the discussions they already had with Laffitte. To avoid as much risk as possible, the Mint was planning to move five million dollars worth of gold coins and ingots by water to the Port of Shreveport, and then by train to San Francisco. Plans were to deposit the gold on the steamboat Mississippi Jazz. It would travel down the Mississippi River to the Gulf of Mexico and then West to where the Atchafalaya River spilled in to the Gulf near Morgan City. From there they would travel up the Atchafalaya to an area near Simmesport where the Red River flowed into this mighty River. Once on the Red River the Mississippi Jazz would travel to the Port of Shreveport.

The CoCo Bed Kid was intrigued by the plan and tactics used to ensure the safety of this mission. Being an old seafaring Pirate, Laffitte's mouth was watering about the contact with another ship.

David and Paul could both see their Cousin, the old Pirate's enthusiasm, but had to smilingly tell him to just hold on and listen to the rest of the story. Upriver from Simmesport was the Port of Alexandria, about halfway to the Port of Shreveport. In Alexandria there was an oddity about the Red River. At certain times of the year water levels dropped to a level that interrupted northbound traffic. Everyone had to wait until the rainy season to put water into the Red River to raise its level and resume boat traffic.

This would be the perfect spot to attack the Mississippi Jazz and plunder the gold. Alexandria was still rebuilding from being virtually burned down after the Union Army traveled through it during the Civil War. Security would be limited giving Laffitte and his men the perfect opportunity with little resistance. From information that the Carr's had from their men inside the Mint, plans were to move the gold in three days. Unknown to officials inside the Mint, the Red River water level at the Port of Alexandria was at its lowest stage and there was already a bottle neck of river traffic at that location. This was the time to strike.

CHAPTER 10

After their meeting was concluded, the Carrs invited the Kid, Murrell, and their Cousin Jean Laffitte to Janice's Place for a nightcap. As they entered the Bar, Murrell spotted his men sitting at a table with Janice. As the group walked over to join them, Janice rose and asked one of her waitresses to bring some additional chairs. When they were all seated, Janice happened to be next to the CoCo Bed Kid and gave him one her infectious smiles. The Kid was tongue tied and could only smile back. Janice told her partners that Dennis, Jerry, and Yonie had kept her entertained by telling of some of their dangerous exploits. She had a few of her own but chose not to share them.

After a couple of drinks everyone decided that it was time to retire. It had been a long day since leaving Galveston that morning. It was agreed to meet in the restaurant early the next morning for coffee and beignets and continued discussions would be held about their upcoming mission.

The accommodations were luxurious and everyone slept soundly. The Kid's last image before falling into a peaceful sleep was the smile of Janice Adkins.

After everyone was comfortably seated in a private area of the restaurant, all of the men were served delicious dark roast coffee and sugar powdered beignets.

After they had left the others the night before, the Carrs returned to their office and met their two trusted employees who worked at the New Orleans Mint. It was decided that the two men would go back to the Mint under the cover of darkness and retrieve enough Mint Uniforms for the Kid, Murrell, and his men. It had been decided that these men would board the Mississippi Jazz in a couple of days and travel as tourists, only to utilize the Mint Uniforms as cover when time came for them to steal the gold shipment. David would not know until later in the day about arrangements he and Paul had made to obtain a small steamboat for Laffitte and his men to make the voyage to Alexandria ahead of the gold shipment. Once there they would survey the situation and make plans to join up with the Kid, Murrell, and his men who would be traveling on the Mississippi Jazz Steamboat.

All of this information was related to the Kid, Murrell, and his men over breakfast. They were impressed with the Carrs planning and helpfulness. Of course they expected to be very handsomely compensated once the mission was successfully completed. David told them to make themselves at home and that they would all meet in his office later during the day. He should have their uniforms by then and confirmation that a boat had been secured for Laffitte and his men. The sooner that he and his men left for Alexandria the better. Time was at a point where rain would be dumped into the Red River, allowing boat traffic to resume. A hurricane was baring down on the New Orleans area and should make landfall in a couple of days. Right after the departure of the Mississippi Jazz, rainfall from the hurricane would pound Southern and Central Louisiana.

CHAPTER 11

With the clever disguise Laffitte had made up for himself he could easily walk the streets of New Orleans and no one would recognize him. For this reason David Carr invited his Cousin to accompany him to the Shipyard to see what his men had come up with in terms of a boat.

During the battle at Forts Jackson and Philip one of the Union Navy's Gunboats was seriously damaged and later brought to the shipyard in New Orleans for repairs. During the early stages of the Civil War the Union had contracted shipbuilders in Scotland and England to construct blockade runners which were designed for speed and undetectability at night. These ironclad Gunboats were also equipped with spar torpedoes. The Union Navy's Gunboat Itasco was one damaged during the battle attempting to break the blockade. It had been repaired and was sea worthy, although had never been taken from the shipyard. With the impending hurricane, Carr planned to introduce his Cousin as an old sea Captain from Europe who could take the Itasco out of New Orleans for a trial run as well as to protect her from expected high water from the upcoming storm. David's men had made these arrangements with the Port Management early that morning and it was now time for introductions to be made for Laffitte to take command of the Gunboat.

When The CoCo Bed Kid, along with John Murrell and his men, met with Laffitte and the Carrs in their office at the arranged meeting time, arrangements for the Gunboat had been completed. Laffitte and his men would take control of the Itasco in a couple of hours. They planned to cruise back down the Mississippi River to the mouth of the Gulf of Mexico, and then travel West to the mouth of the Atchafalaya near Morgan City, then travel up to Simmesport, and then to the Port of Alexandria, where they would then begin scouting the area and making plans for the Mississippi Jazz's arrival.

Paul Carr had news from the New Orleans Mint as well. Due to the hurricane that was baring down on New Orleans, the Mississippi Jazz was to depart the Port the next morning to escape the storms wrath. Workers from the Mint would be loading the gold shipment in the early hours of the morning under heavy security. Only ten security guards would accompany the shipment on the Mississippi Jazz.

Paul then presented the Kid, Murrell, Dennis, Jerry, and Yonie with their Mint Security Uniforms that his men had procured the night before. It was going to be a busy afternoon. Paul told them that he would arrange for tickets on the Jazz for their men, as well as making arrangements to have their horses moved from Laffitte's ship to the Jazz.

Laffitte and his men would return to their ship to pick up additional supplies and then take control of the Gunboat Itasco and depart in a couple of hours. The

Kid, along with Murrell and his men would gather their possessions from their rooms and wait on Laffitte's ship until boarding time for the Mississippi Jazz came in the morning. Best wishes were passed all around for a successful mission.

CHAPTER 12

In the meantime, as these plans were unfolding in New Orleans, a meeting of another kind was taking place at the Port of Alexandria, where more vessels were being halted, both Northbound as well as Southbound due to the low water level in the Red River.

In the office of Port Authority Chairman Robert Porter discussions were being held with a committee Porter had assembled to address the need of dredging the Red River to alleviate the annual issue of low water level and economic loss due to it.

Porter told the assembled men that he had sent word to the owner of a dredging company in Shreveport named Terry Johnson. His company had a stellar reputation for work they had done on the Mississippi River and other bodies of water throughout the State. Porter said that he assumed Johnson would wait to see what the impending hurricane would do. All they could do now was wait.

With the hurricane churning toward the Gulf of Mexico and possibly New Orleans, Terry Johnson, owner of Johnson Dredging Company and his partner Sparky, had to cancel their plans to meet with Port Authority Chairman Robert Porter at the Port of Alexandria, to begin discussions of dredging the Red River there. By dredging this mighty River, it would allow boat traffic, both North and South, that had been halted during drought seasons when the River was as its lowest point, to continue their voyages. When they were halted by the low water in the Red River, it caused a tremendous economic burden for merchants from the Port of Shreveport, through Alexandria, Baton Rouge, to New Orleans. Many times entire shipments of produce was lost, and many times when livestock was being transported, they lost weight, even though being fed, but lack of activity from crowded conditions left them in poor health.

Johnson had completed successfully, projects along the Mississippi River from New Orleans down to the Gulf of Mexico, and a project such as the Red River dredging at the Port of Alexandria would be a simple project for Terry, Sparky, and their professional and talented crew they had working for them.

Johnson knew that he could make another small fortune for his partner and company by opening the Red River for uninterrupted river traffic. Terry was unaware of the impending robbery that the CoCo Bed Kid, John Murrell, and Jean Laffitte had in mind. If the robbery was as successful as the CoCo Bed Kid figured it would be, Terry Johnson and his partner Sparky would have no problem in securing a good lucrative contract from the Port of Alexandria authorities to dredge the Red River in their area.

CHAPTER 13

Late in the afternoon Jean Laffitte and his men took command of the Gunboat Itasco and were steaming down the Mississippi River toward the Gulf of Mexico. In the Captain's control quarters Laffitte could not believe his good fortune. He had sailed his mighty Warship across several seas and had conquered and plundered many other ships that he had come into contact with. His crew of fierce Pirates and the many cannons they had access to, was too much for even the most challenging encounters.

The sleek design of the Gunboat Itasco made navigation effortless and the two coal burning furnaces provided his Gunboat with amazing speed, and Laffitte marveled at the black smoke that billowed from its two stacks. Although the Itasco was built to break blockades with its reinforced hull of steel, it moved through the water swiftly and created little wake. The craft also displaced little depth in the water and Laffitte was sure that he could navigate through the low water level once he reached the Port of Alexandria and the larger vessels that were forced to dock until the Red River water level rose to a height that would allow them to resume their North and South bound missions.

As the Itasco passed the area where she had been disabled during the Civil War attempting to break the blockade set up by Confederate forces that were assigned to Forts Jackson and Philip, there were few gas lights sparkling at Fort Jackson and none directly across the

Mississippi River where Fort Philip lay in ruin and rubble.

With his assistant navigating the Itasco, the old Pirate stood on her bow as she slowly passed Fort Jackson. He silently said a prayer for the tragic loss of life that took place on both the Confederate and Union sides. The War of Northern Aggression was such a tragic event fought for all the wrong reasons.

When the Gunboat Itasco arrived at the Gulf of Mexico mouth, Laffitte turned her West toward the area where the Atchafalaya River spilled into the Gulf, he could see that waves were beginning to pick up to higher than normal, caused by the impending storm. His thoughts were on his beloved ship that was anchored back in the Port of New Orleans and prayed that she would be spared serious damage. At their current pace Laffitte figured they would arrive at the Port of Alexandria by morning.

As Captain Jean Laffitte was navigating the Itasco into the Port of Alexandria the next morning, the Coco Bed Kid, John Murrell, along with his men Dennis, Jerry, and Yonie, were boarding the Mississippi Jazz for their journey to the Port of Alexandria. As they all stood on the deck of the Jazz as she pulled away from the dock, the wind was beginning to increase from the impending hurricane. The water was beginning to become increasingly choppy as well.

As the New Orleans Jazz began to steam down the Mississippi River toward the Gulf of Mexico, the Kid and Murrell waved goodbye to New Orleans, and hoped their mission would be successful and harm would come to none of them. Just as the emotions felt by Jean Laffitte as he passed Fort Jackson the night before, the Coco Bed Kid felt the same as he stood on the upper deck as they passed by the Fort and said a prayer of his own for the lost souls of that horrible battle.

When the Mississippi Jazz reached the mouth of the Gulf she also turned West as the waves continued to increase and pound at her sides. The storm was really beginning to bare down on the area and the Kid hoped they would be able to outrun it.

After the men returned to their quarters they began discussions of their upcoming mission. They had seen several of the New Orleans Mint security personally walking around, mingling with other passengers on board the Jazz. The Kid and Murrell, after sizing the guards up they were convinced they would pose no problem when it came time to carry out their mission of procuring the gold that the guards were charged with to protect.

Barring any issues Laffitte and his men should already be at the Port of Alexandria. From discussions the Kid had earlier with the Jazz Captain, they should arrive at the Alexandria Port the next morning. Laffitte and his men should have had ample time to scope out the area and prepare for a successful attempt at relieving the Mint Guards of their cargo.

CHAPTER 14

Once they reached the Port of Alexandria, Laffitte discovered that he could easily navigated the Itasco through the low area of the Red River, much to the dismay of Captains on the stranded vessels who were forced to dock. He crossed through the low water and passed a curve in the Red River where Fort Buhlow and Fort Randolph stood. Surveying the area more closely and speaking with fishermen on shore, Laffitte learned that a Bayou named Rigolette ran near Fort Buhlow. Laffitte had a plan as to how this could be a great diversionary point because of its nearness to the downtown Port where the Mississippi Jazz would be forced to dock.

A light rain had begun to fall and the old Pirate Captain knew that he needed to act quickly. He turned the Itasco around and headed back to dock near the Port offices. He first wanted to meet with Port Commissioner Robert Porter to make arrangements to have the Gunboat returned to the Port of New Orleans unharmed. He wanted no problems for his Cousins David and Paul Carr.

Once meeting with Porter, Laffitte laid out a story that was hard to believe even to himself. The reason for his request to return the Itasco was that it was no longer needed for him to use, and after all, he had been doing this as a favor to the Port Commissioner in New Orleans to make sure it was able to navigate successfully after repairs.

Laffitte then related that he had been contracted to supply stone for the railroad from an area near Alexandria. He needed advice as to where he could obtain several teams of horses along with wagons to deliver the stone to his contractor. Laffitte also inquired where he could acquire explosives necessary for gathering the stone.

Robert Porter was happy to oblige their request and said that he could arrange to have the Itasco returned to New Orleans as soon as the weather was favorable. As far as wagons and teams, he conducted that business at the Port and could easily arrange that service for him. As far as the explosives he had an old friend at Fort Buhlow that could satisfy those needs, and if not all, the nearby Fort Randolph could.

Porter gave a bit of background for the two Forts. They had been built during the Civil War to protect the City during the Red River Campaign. They were taken over by the Union Troops; however, and the City was not saved.

Laffitte had introduced himself with a false name and credentials to Robert Porter and it turned out to be successful, and thanked Porter for his assistance. For the time being Laffitte made arrangements for one wagon and team as well as horses for himself and his four men. He excused himself and they picked up a team and returned to the Itasco to get their belongings and headed to Fort Buhlow to acquire the explosives. Fortunately the rain had not increased and they were sure the Red River would not rise high enough by morning to allow traffic to begin navigating again.

After they loaded their belongings into the wagon, Laffitte told his men that they could move the boxes of gold which would be taken off the Mississippi Jazz, and then make their getaway. He would leave their destination after the robbery to the CoCo Bed Kid and John Murrell.

They then headed to Fort Buhlow to make arrangements for the explosives they would need for Laffitte's other plan. They would find a place on Bayou Rigolette to set off a huge explosion that would be a distraction which would bring people and the authorities from the dock. Everyone thought this was a clever idea.

Again they encountered no resistance once they met with the Commander at Fort Buhlow for the explosives. Robert Porter had sent a courier ahead informing his old friend, the Commander, of their needs. After four barrels of black powder and fuses were loaded into the wagon, Laffitte and his men rode over to Bayou Rigolette in search of a good spot to place the black powder. It did not take long to find a secluded spot along the Bayou where all four barrels of black powder was concealed from the rain as well as anyone who may pass the area.

Even though they wore their sea worthy rain gear, the men were getting wet and tired. They headed their team back to a stable near the Port where the animals would be fed and cared for, until needed again.

Mr. Porter had told his mysterious friend about a Hotel which was about halfway in construction but was taking guests in some of their completed rooms. Once finished, the Bentley Hotel would be one of the finest in the South. Porter had sent word to arrange for rooms that his important guests would need.

Once they had settled in their rooms and had a hot bath and dressed in dry clothing, Laffitte and his men met in the makeshift restaurant and ordered a fine meal. It was nearing darkness and the rain was picking up. All Laffitte and his men needed to do now was wait until morning for the arrival of the Mississippi Jazz that was carrying the CoCo Bed Kid, John Murrell, and his men. Their part of the work had been done and it was time for a good night's sleep after their delicious meal.

Chapter 15

It had been an uneventful night and the CoCo Bed Kid and his traveling companions were able to get a good night's sleep on the Mississippi Jazz in preparation for tomorrow's big day. Just before dawn the Jazz was pulling into her spot at the dock and the crewmen were securing the mighty vessel.

The Kid joined Murrell and his men in the lavish dining room. They were all in a jovial mood and one would never know that they may soon pull off the heist of a lifetime, if everything went well. Everyone had to be prepared, there was no room for error. This would be a coordinated effort between the Kid, Murrell, and Laffitte.

It wasn't long after the New Orleans Jazz was secured at the dock when one of the Laffitte pirates found the men and brought everyone back to the unfinished Hotel Bentley. Everyone was assembled except one of Laffitte's trusted men, Noah Johnson, who had volunteered to scout the getaway route if the robbery was successfully pulled off.

Well before dawn Laffitte had sent Noah across the Red River to explore an escape route once the wagon was loaded with the many crates of gold coins and ingots. Noah talked with several old men at the dock about an exploration mission that he was making for some friends. He wondered what lay ahead along the Red River route. It was explained to Johnson that upriver there was a small community that served the needs of the massive

Calhoun Plantation. It was one of the largest in the area and there was a lot of racial strife there during and after Reconstruction. Near Colfax there was a ferry that crossed the Red River. It was mainly used to transport the Calhoun Plantation cotton to nearby cotton gins in the Village of Cloutierville, as well as others who wanted to escape the violence that cropped up at times. As Noah digested this information he smiled. He remembered the CoCo Bed Kid saying something about being from the Cloutierville area.

With this information in hand Noah hurried back to the hotel. He arrived just as the others were finishing breakfast. Murrell and the Kid only had coffee since they were still full from their own breakfast on the Jazz.

Laffitte ordered Noah breakfast and coffee as he joined them at the table. After he was seated, with a cup of hot coffee in hand, Noah began to relate the information that he had uncovered. The CoCo Bed Kid listened intently and he was impressed with young Noah Johnson's knowledge and enthusiasm.

CHAPTER 16

After Noah Johnson had completed the story of his mission, everyone agreed that this would make an excellent escape plan. The CoCo Bed Kid was especially pleased since it would bring him back near his Cloutierville home near CoCo Bed. He was equally impressed with young Noah because he was going to need a strong and intelligent person to help him after he received his share of the gold robbery. The Kid could not help but see the eyes of those poor black people, as well as white, as he was leaving CoCo Bed Road a few weeks earlier. What the Kid had in mind for his money would really make him a Robin Hood in the eyes of those on CoCo Bed. John Murrell was also impressed with this plan because it would bring him closer to his hideout near Wolf Rock Cave. Now to plan how they were going to get the gold.

Jean Laffitte was now in a position to release another piece of important information. Before they left New Orleans, his Cousin David Carr told him that his men who were imbedded at the New Orleans Mint, the same ones who provided the Mint Security Uniforms, had also arranged with the Mint Manager to have a relief crew replace those guarding the cargo when they reached the Port of Alexandria, before the Mississippi Jazz continued her voyage to the Port of Shreveport. Included with the fake uniforms were professionally made documents of authenticity for the outlaw crew who would be replacements. They would present these papers to the guards they were to replace, and it should not be an issue, because the guards would be anxious for a return to New Orleans considering the storm that was going to cause a threat perhaps to their families. If things went well, the robbery could go off without a hitch without a shot being fired.

The men all made their way back to the Mississippi Jazz in the pouring rain. The storm had reached the Louisiana coast near Calcasieu Pass. Although it had not reached hurricane strength it brought high gusting winds and torrential rain to the South and Central Louisiana areas. An English Schooner by the name of Agness had been washed ashore near Calcasieu Lake receiving severe damage and injuries to her crew. Laffitte was concerned about his Schooner docked at the Port of New Orleans; however, there was nothing that he could do about it.

When they were finally able to board the Jazz and dry off from the heavy rain, more plans were made. Laffitte and his men were then able to get the CoCo Bed Kid and Murrell's horses offloaded from the Jazz and brought to the corral where their horses and the wagon had been stored.

Plans were for Noah Johnson to stay with the Kid and Murrell until it was time for the heist. About an hour before, he was to depart the Mississippi Jazz, make his way back to the corral for his horse, and then head out to Bayou Rigolette and set off the black powder, creating the huge explosion they all hoped would draw a lot of people, as well as law enforcement personnel. After Johnson had set the fuses he was to take the River Road out of town to a safe point and wait for the Kid and Murrell's escape from the area.

Once the explosion went off there would be chaos. People would be rushing to the area leaving the new Mint Security Guards to carry out their mission. Should anyone question them, a good cover story had been arranged. With their credentials, the Kid could just tell anyone who asked that they were just trying to protect their cargo, not knowing what the explosion was all about. It was also a plus that no one knew that there was gold in the crates.

It was now time for the new security guards to retire to their respective rooms to property dress in their New Orleans Mint Security Uniforms. Well wishes for safety and success were passed around by all, with the knowledge that by nightfall everyone would have wealth beyond imagination.

CHAPTER 17

After Laffitte and his men were dry and comfortable at the corral, discussions were held in regard to the next days activities after the gold shipment was secure. Laffitte was going to let young Noah Johnson travel with the CoCo Kid and John Murrell, to a point where they would divide up the loot. He trusted Noah and would instruct him of his intentions when he stopped by the corral later to pick up his horse. From there he would head over to where the black powder was stored on Bayou Rigolette and detonate the explosives. He would travel to Galveston with their share as soon as that transition was completed.

There was a railroad in Alexandria that traveled to New Orleans called the New Orleans Pacific Railroad. Originally called the Ralph Smith Smith Railroad, and then the Alexandria Cheneyville Railroad, it was the first railroad built West of the Mississippi River during the 1800's. They finally sold out to the New Orleans syndicate and had operated successfully ever since.

Laffitte sent one of his men to the railroad station with money to purchase tickets for their return trip to New Orleans. He was anxious to get back to see if his beloved Schooner had received any damage during the storm. Everyone was satisfied to let Noah Johnson get their share of the gold and return to Galveston with it. In their minds they were already spending the loot.

CHAPTER 18

David
Carr
"17"

Aboard the Mississippi Jazz the CoCo Bed Kid suggested they all meet in John Murrell's room for further discussion on how they would implement the guard switch. The Kid suggested they return to their rooms at the unfinished Bentley Hotel. Murrell had wisely held their rooms when they left earlier. He thought it would make for better optics if they boarded the Jazz wearing their Mint Uniforms. This was agreed to by all involved. Once this plan was agreed to, the Kid, Murrell, Dennis, Jerry, and Yonie, along with Noah Johnson, left the Jazz in the slackening rain and headed to the Bentley. They would dress in their uniforms and wait until four-thirty and return to the Mississippi Jazz and relieve the Mint Guards at five o'clock. Knowing that the crew change would be short and sweet, it was agreed that Noah would pick up his horse at the stables and make his way to Bayou Rigolette to the place where the black powder was hidden. He was also instructed to have the team and wagon waiting at the gangplank of the Jazz at seven o'clock sharp.

Time seemed at a standstill, but four thirty finally arrived and all the men, dressed in their crisp New Orleans Mint Uniforms, made their way back to the Mississippi Jazz. Surprisingly the rain had stopped.

The CoCo Bed Kid and his group had no problems as they made their way to the cargo room and knocked on the door. It was opened by the lead guard and they were allowed to enter. They all had their phony papers in hand and passed them on to the lead guard and he looked them over and nodded acceptance. They all introduced each other and the real guards were excited about seeing their relief. All wanted a return to New Orleans and their families, Praying no injuries had occurred during the storm. Over in a corner, covered with a tarp, sat eight large crates of gold coins and ingots. There was also a four wheeled dolly that would be used to move the crates once the Jazz arrived at the Port of Shreveport. Two crates at a time could fit on the dolly. The setup was agreeable to the Kid and Murrell, and it would soon meet their needs. Without further conversation the tired guards rushed out to the dock. Their plans were to board the six o'clock New Orleans Pacific Railroad Train and return home. Jean Laffitte and his men would also be on that same train.

Since the cargo room door would not be unlocked for any reason, the tarp was pulled from the crates of gold and two were loaded on to the dolly. The crates were heavy and all of the men smiled. In less than two hours Noah Johnson would be setting off the explosives. All they could do now was patiently wait.

CHAPTER 19

Since it was such a short distance to Bayou Rigolette where the black powder was hidden, Noah Johnson decided to return to the corral where Jean Laffitte and his friends were, and see them off on the six o'clock train to New Orleans. Arrangements had already been made to have the team of horses and the wagon at the dock near the Mississippi Jazz by seven o'clock. Once Laffitte and his friends were safely on the train Noah planned to head straight to Bayou Rigolette.

Back in the cargo room aboard the Jazz, The CoCo Bed Kid and John Murrell we're discussing their getaway plans. Once the explosion drew curious people from the dock, they would begin loading the crates of gold and bring them to the waiting wagon. It should not be hard to find River Road. From there they would set out and meet Noah Johnson along the way. From what they had learned it was about a four hour ride to the little town of Colfax where they would take the ferry across Red River. Once on the other side they would travel to the little settlement of Marco, where they would find a good place to divide the gold shipment. Noah would then proceed to Chopin where he would take a train which would take him to Galveston, where he would meet Jean Laffitte, who would be on his way from New Orleans on his ship. The CoCo Bed Kid said that he planned a return to the Village of Cloutierville, and return to his old burned out home place on CoCo Bed. John Murrell indicated that he wanted to return to their hideout at the Wolf Rock

Cave to clean out his belongings. He suggested that Dennis, Jerry, and Yonie do the same. Murrell told his men that they could take this opportunity to go their own way and perhaps settle down comfortably with their new found wealth. As for John Murrell, he said that he wanted to return to his home near Williamson County, Tennessee and settle down. He was tired of being on the run all the time, and being known as the great western land pirate was taking its toll. The mood of all the men being in this room full of gold was festive. They could not want until seven o'clock.

It was nearing six o'clock when Jean Laffitte and his men made their way to the train station and boarded the New Orleans bound train. The New Orleans Mint Security crew had boarded right before them. Before he left the corral Laffitte had paid the owner a generous sum to make sure the team and wagon was at the Mississippi Jazz a little before seven o'clock. Not long after they were all seated, Laffitte heard the Conductor announce "All Aboard", and the train began to move out slowly from the station.

Back on Bayou Rigolette, Noah Johnson was concealed in the trees near the barrels of black powder. He had already laid out his fuses and was prepared to light them. His horse was tied up near him, and he continued to look at his pocket watch.

Back in the cargo room of the Mississippi Jazz, The CoCo Bed Kid was watching his pocket watch as it ticked down to seven o'clock. About that time they felt the Jazz tremor and shake as they simultaneously heard an ear splitting explosion that filled the night. It was time for them to get to work.

CHAPTER 20

Although everyone was anxious to begin moving the gold, the Kid suggested they wait about fifteen minutes to allow the curious and excited people on board to thin out a little. The wait was excruciating but they finally opened the cargo door and began to pull the heavy dolly out to the area where the elevator was located that would bring them to the second deck where the gang plank was located. There was still a lot of panic and excitement aboard the Mississippi Jazz; however, it had somewhat subsided. As they made their way to the exit one of the crewmen stopped them and inquired as to where they were going. Murrell said that there had been a change in plans and they were instructed to take the cargo to the train station. Plans were to depart from there to the Port of Shreveport where another crew would accompany the cargo to San Francisco. No one knew what the cargo contained. The crewmen were satisfied and actually cleared the bystanders so they could make their way to the waiting wagon. As they were departing, the Kid casually asked what the explosion was about, but they had no answer. After the first two crates were loaded on to the wagon, Murrell left Yonie in charge of its safekeeping, as they returned to the Jazz, and with the crewmen's capable assistance transferred the remaining six crates very quickly. The Kid thanked them and provided a substantial tip, for which they were grateful. One of the crewmen told them the directions to River Road before he returned to his duties on the Jazz.

As they slowly made their way to River Road the Kid asked several bystanders if they knew the cause of the explosion. No one seemed to know the cause but all agreed there had been no injuries. It did not take long for the little expedition to reach River Road and they turned West in hopes they would meet up with Noah very soon.

Through the moonlit night they were able to make good time and soon spotted a rider on horseback in front of them. It was Noah Johnson.

They all greeted him happily and told Noah that he had done a wonderful job, and their understanding was that no one was hurt, for which Noah was grateful.

Since it would be near midnight when they neared Colfax, they decided it would be best to make camp outside of town and find the ferry in the morning after they had breakfast. Knowing they were all wealthy men, one more night sleeping on the ground didn't bother them as they made their way up the road.

It was nearing midnight as they approached the flickering gas lamps of Colfax in the distance. The Kid asked Noah if he would scout around to find them a suitable camping spot. He quickly found a grove of trees that would be suitable and very concealing. As they pulled the team and wagon off the road into the grove of trees, shots rang out in the distance. It was assumed the they came from Colfax. Everyone was then on alert and Noah told them of what he had learned about Colfax. Since reconstruction, years before, there had been trouble between the Calhoun Plantation and the poor farmers, as well as the freed black slaves, about the poor living conditions they had to endure. Sporadic riots broke out and this was probably one of them. Many lives had been lost and sadly they were from the poor people. The CoCo Bed Kid thought about the sad look in the eyes of old people as he was leaving CoCo Bed a couple of weeks earlier. As he was preparing his bedroll he knew how part of his fortune would be spent. He would by the Estate which owned the land occupied by CoCo Bed, and he knew how he would explain how he amassed his fortune.

CHAPTER 21

By the time everyone had found a place to set up their bedrolls, and after rubbing down their horses and giving them a ration of oats, shooting in the distance had stopped. It was decided that building a fire would be too dangerous, so everyone had a cold supper of dried jerky. Noah Johnson had certainly found them a good camping spot, nestled in a secluded grove of trees with a cool little stream running by them.

It was nearing daybreak as the men began to stir and smell the brewing coffee as well as the sound of frying bacon on the small fire that Noah and Yonie had put together. They had risen early and felt that it was safe enough to build a fire and make breakfast for the men. It would be a treat after last night's cold supper.

As the men enjoyed their coffee and breakfast the mood was jovial. John Murrell had already made his announcement of retirement, while the others were boasting of their future plans. The CoCo Bed Kid was the only one who had not discussed his plans, but as he was repeatedly being asked, he decided to let them know. The Kid told those assembled of his vision to purchase the CoCo Bed property from the Estate that held it. This had been his home and where his heart was. His mother and father were buried near their burned out home that he had been born in. With his fortune he planned to build a lavish home and replace the old shotgun shacks that were inhabited by the poor black and white men who had worked as sharecroppers their entire lives for the Estate, and had little or nothing to show for it. They deserved to spend their remaining days in relative comfort. The Kid described the beauty of the area, upon which stood vast amounts of tall virgin timber, with an abundance of game that ran through the area. The rich red soil produced an abundance of cotton, corn, and wheat. The place was a sight to see.

Dennis and Jerry were spellbound as they listened to the CoCo Bed Kid tell his story. Since John Murrell had already given his intention of retirement and disbanding the gang, they were intrigued with the prospect of joining the Kid and his vision. With their combined fortunes, and that of his, a dynasty could be in the making. Dennis and Jerry proposed that they would love to join the Kid if he would be interested in their services. The Kid laughed and asked if they felt the idea of farming was in their blood, after a life of being hunted outlaws. The young men laughed and said that it may not be that exciting, but would certainly allow them to live much longer lives. The Coco Bed Kid laughed and shook hands with his new partners.

After their breakfast utensils had been cleaned and put away, the horses fed and saddled, the wagon hitched to its team, it was now time to ride into Colfax and locate the ferry.

CHAPTER 22

Not long after they had reached Colfax, the group of men were told the location of the ferry, which was nearby. Once reaching the ferry John Murrell approached its operator who was shoveling coal into the bin that would power the ferry's engine that would enabled it to cross the Red River and make a return trip. It appeared they would be the first customers of the day. Murrell approached the operator and introduced himself. The operator said that his name was David Stamey and that he had been operating the ferry for several years. Prior to this he had been the school teacher at a small building on the Calhoun Plantation to educate the young children of those families who worked there. He decided to leave when unrest between the community and the Plantation had turned violent.

Stamey instructed Murrell to have his men and wagon board and move to the front of the ferry, leaving room for another wagon that he saw fast approaching. Murrell did as instructed and waved his people aboard. By the time they were settled, the other wagon had arrived, and as the men were frantically telling the operator that they were being chased by some people from the Calhoun Plantation, and feared for their lives. Stamey urged them aboard and began unfastening the mooring lines.

As the big ferry slowly began to make her way across the Red River, the riders began firing shots toward the ferry. Stamey had installed steel plates on board for just this purpose, and instructed everyone to get behind them. He had built one shield for himself as well and stood behind it as he powered up the ferry engine.

Bullets began to ring off the steel plates as the two men from the ferry began to return fire. Two women and four small children found shelter behind one of the steel plates as well. The CoCo Bed Kid, along with John Murrell and his men, began to return fire as well. They saw two men on the bank fall near their horses. As they neared the middle of Red River, Murrell noticed that Yonie was holding his shoulder and saw blood seeping from between his fingers. As Murrell cautiously made his way toward Yonie he was waved off. Yonie said that he was all right. Shots continued to ring out as the ferry was beginning to move out of range. Before they had moved much further, and as shots continued to ring out from the bank, Dennis fell from a wound himself. The CoCo Bed Kid rushed to his side and gave aid to his new found friend, as Noah Johnson was already putting bandages on Yonie's wound to prevent the flow of blood. Murrell and the two new passengers continued to fire toward the opposite bank as David Stamey by now had the engine at full speed as they began getting closer to the Red River bank. The Kid had finished putting a bandage on Dennis. His wound was on the right side of his chest. Neither of the men appeared to have life threatening injuries; however, it was essential to get the loss of blood stopped.

They finally reached the ferry landing point and the Kid and Murrell began to move their wagon and the horses off the ferry, as the newcomers followed behind them. Jerry took control of Dennis and Yonie's horses, as well as Noah's, who was caring for the injured men.

When all were safely on the bank, the ferry operator David Stamey said that he was finished. This violence was more than he could deal with. He told the others that he wished he could burn the ferry since it was owned by the Calhoun Plantation. Noah Johnson smiled as he walked to his horse and retrieved a package from his saddlebags. Back on Bayou Rigolette, he had saved about five pounds of the black powder and some fuses. He knew that he would have enough black powder to set off the explosion that was necessary. He figured this would come in handy at some point, and this was the time. Noah showed the black powder to Stamey and said he would be happy to do the honors. Both men laughed, and as Noah was preparing the charge, Stamey was engaging the engine for a return trip across the Red River. When Noah gave the signal that the fuse had been lit, he quickly jumped off the ferry as David engaged the gear and did the same. Not long after the ferry had left the bank, a small blast sounded, and the ferry was engulfed in flame. They all cheered as the ferry sunk about halfway across the Red River.

Once this matter had been settled the Kid asked Stamey where the nearest Doctor was located. David had indicated there was two excellent Doctors in Marco, which was much nearer than the Village of Cloutierville.

David Stamey said that Dr. Debbie Walker and Dr. Shelby Borders had earned their degrees from John Hopkins Medical School in Baltimore, Maryland a couple of years before. They had graduated near the top of their class and wanted to return and set up a practice together near where they had grown up. Stamey said they were excellent Doctors, and the two injured men would receive excellent care.

After this discussion and plans were made for Marco, the Kid asked the men from the escaped wagon what their plans were. He was told that they had been working on the Calhoun Plantation, and like David Stamey, were tired of the violence. They planned to find a new place to become sharecroppers. Without giving any indication of his intentions, the CoCo Bed Kid gave them a nice sum of money and said that he would like for them to find the Gallien Boarding House in Cloutierville, and tell Mrs. Gallien that the CoCo Bed Kid had sent them. He asked David Stamey what his plans were and was told that he planned to make a trip to Natchitoches and see if his old friend Sheriff Vic Jones had anything for him. At the sound of Sheriff Jones name, John Murrell and the Kid shuddered. David asked if he could accompany the families to Cloutierville and they agreed.

It was now time to get Dennis and Yonie to Doctors Debbie Walker and Shelby Borders Office in Marco.

Thankfully, for the injured men, it would be a short journey. As they set out with the injured men, the Kid thanked Stamey and wished him good luck. He also told the families to stay put at the Boarding House until his return. He had a proposition for them.

CHAPTER 23

After the two wounded men were loaded into the wagon and made as comfortable as possible, the CoCo Bed Kid and John Murrell urged the team of horses and wagon down the road toward Marco. David Stamey had told the Kid that Doctor Debbie Walker And Doctor Shelby's Office was the first building on the right as they entered town. Thankfully the ride was smooth so as not to cause too much discomfort for Dennis and Yonie as they lay in the back of the wagon. The group of men soon arrived in Marco and saw the Doctors Office with a white shingle which displayed the names, Doctor Debbie Walker and Doctor Shelby Borders. As the Kid rushed into the office to alert the Doctors of his injured friends, Murrell and Noah began to carefully get Dennis and Yonie out of the wagon and into the building. Doctor Walker ushered Dennis into a room to attend to his wound, and Doctor Borders did the same with Yonie. When the Kid first introduced himself to Doctor Walker he inquired if she had a place they could privately bring their cargo and rest for the night. She pointed to a large barn next to her building and said to utilize it as though their own. Once the two Doctors began working on their two patients, Murrell instructed Noah Johnson to bring the team to the barns front door. After Jerry had the two big doors open, Noah slowly urged the team in. There was just enough room for the horses and wagon behind them to enter the barn. Jerry closed and bolted the doors after the Kid and Murrell had entered.

Confident that Doctor Walker and Doctor Borders would provide professional care to both Dennis and Yonie, he returned to the barn. John Murrell then suggested that each of the four men assembled would take two of the crates and begin counting the gold. Fortunately the gold coins were of high denomination, and the ingots were relatively the same size. Someone at the Mint had put a set of scales in each of the crates, apparently to weigh the ingots. This proved to be a big help in determining the value of their heist. They could weigh several ingots, get an average weight, and assess a value for each by current gold prices. All four men had big smiles on their faces as they ran their fingers through the gold coins and ingots. After several ingots were weighed, Murrell gave the men a price for each and told them to begin counting as he returned to his crates. Another thing that helped in computing their wealth was that all of the gold coins were valued at one hundred dollars each.

As the morning wore on and the counting continued, the Kid decided to step over to the Doctors Office to check the status of their friends. Doctor Walker indicated that things were going smoothly. She would check with her partner Doctor Borders, but felt that his patient was doing fine as well. Satisfied, the Kid returned to the barn and resumed counting the gold coins and ingots in his crates. By late evening their counting was nearly completed and the men were tired, when a knock came from the barn's outer door. Cautiously the Kid answered, and it was Doctor Walker who told him that both of their friends were doing well, and that a short visit was in order if they wished. It was decided that the Kid would remain with the gold while the others visited Dennis and Yonie.

Both men lay in small beds, and though a bit groggy, smiled when they saw their friends enter the room. As Murrell pressed a hundred dollar gold piece in each of their hands, the smiles lit up the room. One would not think they were recovering from serious gunshot wounds.

Murrell asked Doctor Borders when his men could be moved and he said that after a good night's rest they could leave the next day, if ridden in the wagon so as not to jar the stitches in their wounds. Doctor Walker told Murrell that the barn would be at their disposal for as long as they needed it. Murrell thanked her and asked how long she and Doctor Borders had been in practice. She said they had only been practicing there for a year after graduating from John Hopkins Medical School.

She had hoped there would be a Hospital that she and Doctor Borders could become connected with; however, Natchitoches and Alexandria had the only Hospitals in the area. There was basically no Doctors to treat those in the rural areas, so they decided to begin their practice in Marco. It was fulfilling for them to provide the medical help needed in the community. This small

Clinic was essential. Murrell asked what would it cost to build a fully equipped Hospital. Doctor Walker laughed and said there was probably not enough money in all the surrounding Parishes to make that happen. Murrell thanked her and returned to the barn accompanied by Noah and Jerry. The CoCo Bed Kid then took his turn to visit Dennis and Yonie.

The day seemed to fly by and it was nearing darkness when the Kid suggested that Noah Johnson go down the street to a small cafe that Doctor Walker had told him about, and bring them all back a good supper. They had not eaten since early morning, and the day had certainly been an eventful one. They all agreed that the gold counting would be completed before turning in for the night. So far they had counted over six million dollars and still had more to add to that number. This was far more than the original number they had been told the shipment would contain. No one was going to complain about that. They had all the money they would ever spend.

It was not long before Noah returned with eight dinners. He had brought food back for Doctor Walker and Doctor Borders, as well as two light meals for Dennis and Yonie. Everyone else had a huge plate of fried chicken and huge biscuits with butter and honey. The Doctors thanked Noah and said to tell his friends to rest well. They would make sure their patient friends would be fine. Noah asked if he could go in to bring their suppers and wish them goodnight. Doctor Walker said that would be fine. Once Noah was inside with Dennis and Yonie's food, he whispered the amount of gold they had counted thus far. Both injured men almost jumped out of bed with joy; however, their wounds brought them back to earth very quickly.

It didn't take long after their meals had been eaten that the men brought their horses to a long water trough running along the opposite side of the barn. After the horses had been watered each was given a liberal ration of oats and then given a rundown. The CoCo Bed Kid made himself a mental note to send Robert Porter at the Port of Alexandria an amount of money to cover the cost of the horses and wagon. After the animals had been taken care of, the men resumed their task of counting and separating the gold coins and ingots. It was nearing midnight when the last coin and ingot was counted. The men were exhausted but extremely happy. Sitting before them was eight and a half million dollars in gold coins and ingots.

Early the next morning the Coco Bed Kid and John Murrell walked over to the Doctors Office. They wanted to see how Dennis and Yonie were doing. Doctor Walker greeted them and said how much she and Doctor Borders enjoyed their meal last night. Doctor Borders walked in and said their friends had made a miraculous improvement since yesterday. They appeared to be tough men, and in fact, he was releasing both of them, providing they traveled comfortably in the wagon wherever their party had planned to go. The Kid assured both Doctors the patients would be well cared for. Dennis and Yonie both appeared to be fit when they appeared in the outer office. Doctor Walker had thoughtfully provided them with new clothes, since their other attire was soaked with blood.

When the men returned to the barn, the Kid filled them in on the gold count. This was beyond everyone's wildest dreams. Murrell then told them of his conversation with Doctor Walker and Doctor Borders the day before concerning a Hospital. Would they not all agree that because of the excellent treatment Dennis and Yonie had been provided, enough money could be given for the cost of a Hospital, equipment, and staff, and make the two Doctors dreams come true. Everyone assembled agreed wholeheartedly.

During this meeting it was also agreed on how to split this fortune. The CoCo Bed Kid, John Murrell and his men, Noah, Dennis, Jerry, and Yonie would each receive one million dollars in gold. Jean Laffitte would receive one million dollars for himself and his men, David Carr and his brother Paul would receive a million dollars, and half million would go to the Carrs men working at the New Orleans Mint. This seemed to be a fair split of the gold fortune based on the risk involved by each person.

John Murrell then told the men of his discussion about a Hospital with Doctor Walker and Doctor Borders. They had estimated the cost of the facility, equipment, and staff would probably be the unimaginable cost of thirty thousand dollars. Would it not follow the CoCo Bed Kid's reputation of being a modern day Robin Hood, as well as his Pay It Forward theory, to give the Doctors thirty thousand dollars of their gold? Everyone readily agreed and calculated that if everyone put fifty of their gold coins into a bag it would satisfy their need for thirty thousand dollars. It was set.

Once the coins were collected the CoCo Bed Kid and Murrell made their way to the Doctors Office with their good news. Fortunately Doctor Walker and Doctor Borders had no patients at the time. The Kid told them they wanted to pay the bill for the excellent treatment their friends had received, as well as the use of their barn, which they would vacate in the morning. The two Doctors consulted with each other, and said that if twenty five dollars seemed fair, the cost of the new clothing would be free. They hoped this would not be too excessive.

The Kid and Murrell smiled at each other and presented the Doctors with the heavy sack of gold coins, and told them it contained thirty thousand dollars, which would cover the cost of their dream. They explained the money was from the sale of a successful gold mine in California, and this was their way of Paying It Forward for their good fortune. Both Doctors were speechless. The Kid and Murrell said they would not take no for an answer, and Prayed Doctor Walker and Doctor Borders would continue their excellent work. The Kid then asked if there was a nice restaurant in town, and would they join them for supper before they left town the next morning. Doctor Walker said the Marco Steak House was the best in their little town. Murrell said they would treat the Doctors to a delicious steak supper tonight, and their two patients would be joining them. Doctor Borders embraced Doctor Walker as she broke into tears of joy.

CHAPTER 24

After a wonderful steak dinner the night before, the men all expressed their gratitude and best wishes to Doctor Debbie Walker and Doctor Shelby Borders. Dennis and Yonie especially thanked them for their excellent treatment. Both men felt great after the successful work done on their gunshot wounds. As the gang departed both Doctors, it was decided they would see them off the next morning. Once the Coco Bed Kid and John Murrell and his men returned to the barn, all were asleep shortly after they fell onto their bedrolls. All were thankful they had fed and watered the animals before they had left for supper.

Early the next morning, Murrell sent Jerry and Noah down to the little cafe to bring them all back breakfast and coffee. He advised them to bring two extra for the Doctors. It had been decided that the wagon would be left for the Doctors to do with as they wished. Murrell and Jerry would take two of the horses with them to the hideout at Wolf Rock Cave. One of the horses would carry Murrell's gold, and the other would be utilized for the modest belongings of Noah, Dennis, and Yonie, as well as his own. He would then return to the Village of Cloutierville where he was to meet the Kid at Gallien's Boarding House.

When Jerry and Noah returned with the breakfasts, everyone met at the Doctors Office and all enjoyed a delicious breakfast. After everyone had enjoyed the delicious meal, the Kid told Doctor Walker and Doctor

Borders how much their professional services were appreciated and hoped their new Hospital would be a success.

Handshakes and hugs were passed all around and the gang left to prepare for their leave. After Murrell and Jerry had left for Wolf Rock Cave, the Kid would head out toward Cloutierville with his injured friends. Noah would depart for Chopin with Jean Laffitte and the Carrs gold, as well as that for their friends embedded at the New Orleans Mint. He would make train connections to Galveston, leave the gold with Laffitte, with instructions to have the Carr gold delivered to them. Noah would then make his way back to Cloutierville to meet up with the Kid, as he had already anticipated a future working with him.

Best wishes and warnings were given to John Murrell and Jerry as they prepared to leave. Sheriff Vic Jones would more than likely still be searching for them. He was a tenacious man and would not give up easily.

The Kid loaded Jerry's gold, along with that of his own, as well as Dennis and Yonie, on the other horse. He waved goodbye to Murrell and Jerry, as he, Dennis, and Yonie, began their journey to Cloutierville. Noah had already begun his journey to Chopin and the train.

As the Kid and his companions headed toward Cloutierville and the Gallien Boarding House, he was thinking about a proposition for his newly met friend David Stamey. He had already indicated to the two families that escaped the Calhoun Plantation thugs, they would have a good future with him on CoCo Bed. The Kid recalled Stamey telling him that he had been an Educator on the Calhoun Plantation. The Kid envisioned a school on CoCo Bed and he hoped Stamey would accept his offer to become the new Head Master of his CoCo Bed School, and planned to offer him a lucrative salary to educate the children of families who would be working on CoCo Bed.

CHAPTER 25

As the CoCo Bed Kid led the way to the Village of Cloutierville with Dennis and Yonie, his thoughts remained with John Murrell and Jerry. He had tried to talk Murrell out of a return trip to the Wolf Rock Cave. What could be there so important that would compel him to take the risk of an encounter with Sheriff Vic Jones and his posse. Murrell now had wealth beyond imagination, so surely a few clothes and perhaps a saddle or two could easily be replaced; however, when Murrell had his mind made up about something, he could not be persuaded to change it. The Kid was worried about Murrell and Jerry. He did feel that Noah would face any danger as he made his way by train to Galveston with the gold for Jean Laffitte and the Carr Brothers. He asked Dennis and Yonie how they felt and the response was a positive one, and that they would have no problem making the trip to Cloutierville and the guests waiting for them at the Gallien Boarding House.

Darkness was fast approaching as Murrell and Jerry arrived at Wolf Rock Cave. They had not seen any signs of the Sheriff and his posse, but felt certain they were being watched. Both men were on full alert. Once at the Cave, Murrell urged his horses into the entrance, followed by Jerry with his animals. The Cave was large and roomy and continued back into the hills surrounding it. Both men dismounted and Jerry built a small fire for their supper. The horses were drinking from a stream running along one of the walls. Murrell was getting grain from a large bin placed on the opposite side. Jerry was about to begin supper when he heard the sound of a horse as well as breaking branches from outside in the darkness. It was Sheriff Jones and his posse. Jerry quickly alerted Murrell who was moving the horses deeper into the Cave. When he returned they both crouched behind a table that was overturned. Jerry quickly put out the fire leaving the big room in darkness just as gunshots rang out from outside, to hear the sound of bullets bouncing off the Cave's rock walls. Both men returned rapid fire which was immediately returned by another volley of shots from outside. Jerry inquired if Murrell had a plan, and fortunately he did. Long ago he had prepared for an event such as this, and had stored two sticks of dynamite and fuses for the purpose of blowing up the entrance and blocking passageway from the outside. The Cave had an exit far from the entrance from which the two men could escape into a grove of trees. The Cave would be narrow but it was large enough for passageway for the men and their horses.

As Murrell was preparing the dynamite Jerry continued firing into the darkness, as shots from the outside continued to pelt the walls of the Cave. Murrell told Jerry to get the horses ready to leave immediately. Jerry complied and had all their horses ready to escape.

Murrell made his way cautiously to near the Cave's entrance cringing at the sound of every shot. Just as he had ignited the fuses and was returning to Jerry, he felt a jolt to his shoulder and a hot burning sensation. He had been hit, and was knocked to his knees. From the torch light Jerry could see Murrell crawling towards him, and rushed to help his friend. About the time he reached his friend, there was a tremendous explosion, and rocks from the wall completely closed the entrance. The horses were spooked but did not run. Jerry helped Murrell to his feet as he inquired about his injury. Murrell said that it hurt but felt that he could go on. Knowing they were in no danger of anyone entering, and that the exit was concealed, Jerry attended to his friend's gunshot wound. The bullet had entered and exited the shoulder and no bones appeared to be broken.

After they had rested for a while, Murrell told Jerry of his plans. It would be too dangerous going to Natchitoches, so the Port of Shreveport was a safer option. Murrell said that he would make arrangements by train a return to his home in Tennessee.

After they had slowly made their way to the exit of the Cave, Murrell wished Jerry well and said that he had enjoyed their adventures together. Jerry agreed with his old boss and also wished him well. He then watched John Murrell ride off in the darkness with the horse carrying his gold following behind. He seemed to be favoring his right shoulder.

Jerry then turned his horse down a little road that would eventually take him to the Village of Cloutierville. He would never see John Murrell again.

CHAPTER 26

As Jerry made his way down the winding trail through the moonlit night, thoughts went back to his old boss and friend John Murrell. He knew how tough he was and yet still said a Prayer that his health would allow him to make his journey to the Port of Shreveport and then on to his Tennessee home. The image of Murrell holding his shoulder still bothered him. Jerry had never been identified in any of the robberies that he and Murrell had been involved in, so he felt that when the CoCo Bed Kid took he, Dennis, and Yonie, on to assist him with his CoCo Bed Plantation, he would be able to enjoy his wealth of gold.

Back at the Village of Cloutierville, the CoCo Bed Kid, along with Dennis and Yonie, were arriving at the Gallien Boarding House as darkness was beginning to set in. It had been a long and tiring ride since leaving Marco, and they had stopped several times to allow the two men to rest from their wounds. Although they were healing, the Kid did not wand to create any complications for them. The Kid noticed that David Stamey was sitting on the gallery with the two farmers from Calhoun Plantation, Nick and Jay Guilbeau, and their wives Sheila and Colleen. All rose to embrace the Kid, Dennis, and Yonie as they approached. Their greetings expressed the gratefulness they shared for the safe journey from Marco. Noah should be safely on a train by now headed toward Galveston, and all Prayed that Jerry and John Murrell had safely made it to Wolf Rock Cave.

Mrs. Gallien approached the Kid and said that she had lots of hot water at the bath house for them to clean up and change. She hoped they were all hungry because she had prepared a meal of her famous hot tamales and meat pies. She would have one of her employees take their horses to the stable for water, grain, and a good rubdown. She then got a couple of her other men to bring their bags to the respective rooms she had reserved for them. The Kid smiled at Dennis and Yonie and said that their gold was in safe hands.

Before they made their way to the bath house, the Kid asked Mrs. Gallien if she would send for Doctor Wink, who had been the Doctor in Cloutierville for many years, who's office was just down the street. He wanted the Doctor to care for Dennis and Yonie's wounds and redress them. Doctor Wink was immediately summoned and arrived shortly thereafter and began to care for his two patients. After he had left all enjoyed a nice soaking bath and dressed in fresh clothing, and then retired to the dining room where everyone else was waiting.

With all having full stomachs, the Kid invited David Stamey and the two Guilbeau brothers to join him in a private room that Mrs. Gallien had arranged for him. The two wives would join Mrs. Gallien and help with supper dishes. Dennis and Yonie decided to head to their rooms for a good nights rest as well as getting relief for their gunshot wounds. Although their wounds were healing nicely according to Doctor Wink, he suggested as much rest as possible for them.

After they were all seated in the private room the Kid got straight to the point. He told them of his plans to buy the CoCo Bed property the next day. He assured them the offer that he was going to make would ensure him that the property would be his. He had made a small fortune in the California gold rush and was ready to spend some of that fortune, and had visions of what he wanted CoCo Bed to become. He would need good men to help work the property for him and offered Nick and Jay Guilbeau jobs. He also told them that he planned to build houses for them and their wives. Both brothers agreed to the CoCo Bed Kid's proposition.

The Kid then turned his attention to David Stamey. He remembered Stamey telling him that he was a former Educator and that would fit in nicely with plans to build a big school building for the youngsters on the Estate that was to become his.

Stamey was flattered by the Kids offer. His heart had always been with educating young children and helping mold them into productive young adults. He asked the Kid if he could take a couple of days to consider this wonderful offer. He had thought of returning to the Smoky Mountains in North Carolina to visit family he had not seen in a number of years. The Kid that that would be fine. It would probably be a couple of months before the school building would be completed. Stamey then asked the Kid if he could bring along a good friend of his, Doug Ireland, to join him at the school. He told the Kid that Ireland would be a valuable asset for the new school project, and knew that he would accept this mission if offered. Between he and Doug Ireland their school would be the best in the Parish. The Kid thought this was a wonderful idea and readily accepted the offer to add Doug Ireland's services.

The Kid was pleased with the progress that he had with this meeting, and told the men to excuse him for a few minutes. He then returned to his room and put five one hundred dollar gold pieces in small bags. When he returned he gave one of the bags to each of the Guilbeau brothers, and two to David Stamey. He wanted one of the bags to go to his friend Doug Ireland. The Kid explained that this was just his way of Paying It Forward for the good fortune that was presented to him. The men were all grateful for this generous display of kindness. The Kid told the Guilbeau's to just relax with their wives for a couple of weeks until their new houses could be built. The Kid then told Stamey that this might be a good time to make that trip to the Smoky Mountains in North Carolina to visit his family there. Everyone was overjoyed at the prospects for their future. The Kid then invited them to join him for a few drinks at the White Elephant. It had been a while since he had seen his old friend Wall Brooks who owned the White Elephant. They all agreed and happily walked up the street to the bar.

CHAPTER 27

After enjoying several drinks, and a good visit with his old friend Wall Brooks at the White Elephant Bar, The CoCo Bed Kid, David Stamey, and the Guilbeau brothers returned to the Gallien Boarding House for a good night's rest. It seemed like ages since the Kid had left Marco that morning with his injured friends Dennis and Yonie. He was excited about the meeting with the CoCo Bed owner the next morning. Mrs. Gallien had contacted him and set up an early morning meeting the next day. This was going to be a glorious day for Cloutierville and the future of Coco Bed.

The next morning, after being seated in the Estate owner's office, and after pleasantries were exchanged, the Kid got down to business. He casually asked if the Coco Bed property could be for sale. The owner smiled and said that he had certainly thought about the idea, considering his advancing age, and the aches and pains that went with it.

The Kid asked what he thought a fair price for the property would be. The owner laughed and asked who would be interested in purchasing that property, and would even have the money to buy it. The CoCo Bed Kid said that he would. Taken back, the owner smiled and presented a figure that he knew the Kid could not afford. The Kid then asked if a five hundred dollar bonus above the asking price would be acceptable and assure him that the deal could be closed. Even an experienced businessman like the owner knew this was a deal that he could not refuse.

The Kid quickly put him at ease by saying that he had amassed a fortune in the California gold fields and that money would be no object. He explained the importance CoCo Bed held for him since his parents were buried there near their burned out home. They had been slaughtered by the Union forces during that senseless War, during the Battle of Monett's Ferry. The Kid was bitter about this; however, this would be the opportunity for making their death mean something to the other poor sharecroppers on CoCo Bed.

The Estate owner, after recovering from his shock, said that he would have the papers drawn up by his friend Judge Lee Posey in Natchitoches. Judge Posey could be here bright and early the next morning with the paperwork to close the deal. Satisfied and elated, the CoCo Bed Kid shook hands with the soon to be former owner of CoCo Bed, and assured him that the money would be here the next morning.

After the Kid returned to the Gallien Boarding House, he called for a private meeting with his new employees. After all were assembled, he stood and looked over the group, which consisted of Dennis and Yonie, David Stamey, Nick Guilbeau and his wife Shelia, and Jay Guilbeau with his wife Colleen. Jerry had yet to return from his journey to Wolf Rock Cave with John Murrell. All Prayed they were not in harms way. Noah

Johnson was probably already in Galveston with the gold for the old Pirate Jean Laffitte and his men, and arrangements would probably have been made to get the share of David Carr and his brother Paul's gold to them.

The CoCo Bed Kid advised those assembled that he would be the new owner of the CoCo Bed property the next morning, and he wanted them all to stand by until construction was to begin on their new homes, and other buildings on CoCo Bed. He told David Stamey that he should make his trip to the Smoky Mountains in North Carolina to have a short visit with his family. The Kid wanted him back to supervise the building of the new school building.

David told the Kid how much that he appreciated this opportunity; however, he had one more request for the Kid to consider. For the proposed new school it had already been decided to bring Stamey's friend Doug Ireland on board, but he wanted to know if he could also bring on a young woman who was an excellent educator herself. She was the product of parents who had devoted their lives to teaching young children. Her name was Ginny VanSickle, and Stamey felt she would fit in perfectly with their plans at the new school with himself and Ireland. The Kid acknowledged this to be a great idea, and assured him that the school would be entirely under his control, and there would be no interference with his decisions. This would be one of the first new improvements to CoCo Bed and the Kid knew there would be many more to come.

The Kid dismissed them all and said that he would be in his room for a while to have a little rest and making plans for the next morning. He did not want to be disturbed because he wanted to work out details for the CoCo Bed purchase, as well as setting up something for construction on his property. He did want them however, to let him know when Jerry arrived. The Kid was anxious to know how his trip with Murrell had turned out.

CHAPTER 28

When Jerry arrived at the Gallien Boarding House, it was in the early hours of the morning. He was exhausted and was soon asleep on a bed of soft straw as soon as he had watered and fed his horse. He had slept peacefully until the stable operator arrived a few hours later. Jerry quickly cleaned up and changed into fresh clothing. He arrived at the dining room just as Mrs. Gallien was serving those sitting around the table large platters of sausage, eggs, biscuits, and delicious gravy, along with fresh honey.

There was little talking as everyone began to enjoy their meal. After breakfast all listened in silence as Jerry outlined what had happened to he and John Murrell after they had arrived at Wolf Rock Cave. It had been a tense experience and had it not been for Murrell's quick thinking, by blowing up the entrance to the cave, they could have been killed or in custody by now. Although injured by the gunshot wound, Jerry felt that Murrell had made his journey to the Port of Shreveport, and was probably on a train to his home in Tennessee. The CoCo Bed Kid listened quietly to Jerry's story and then laid out his story about meeting with the Coco Bed property owner the day before, and plans for purchase of it this morning. He told Jerry to relax with the others for a few days as he planned to conduct some other business after the purchase of CoCo Bed had been completed.

The Kid then walked over to the Estate owner's office, and was ushered into a large room, and then was introduced to Judge Lee Posey. The Kid sat two large bags of gold coins on the owner's desk and was seated.

The Kid had told the owner the previous day, that he wanted the land purchase to also include all of the livestock and farming equipment needed to produce the various crops of cotton, corn, and wheat. He read over the prepared documents and was satisfied with their content, and happily signed his name, officially making CoCo Bed his own. The previous owner and Judge Lee Posey counted the gold coins and found the amount to be precise, along with the extra five hundred dollars he had promised. The Kid shook hands with both men and put his deed carefully into his pocket. He thanked them both and said that he was then going to meet his friend Henry Rachal at the local bank.

The Kid had previously consulted with Henry Rachal about the Coco Bed property. Since Rachal was owner and operator of the largest bank in the area, and he knew that the advice he would receive was financially prudent. The CoCo Bed Kid planned to depot the rest of his gold fortune into Henry's Cloutierville Bank.

The Kid then went back to the corral and saddled up his horse Dolly and set out to the Sang Pour Sang Sawmill and Construction Company. The owners of this business Dwain and John Dempsey Johnson were friends of his, and he wanted to offer them the opportunity to build all of the homes for he and his new partners, as well as the sharecroppers who lived there, and the new school house as well.

John Dempsey handled the logging part of the business, as well as milling of the timber that had been cut. Dwain and his son Eddie James DeRamus handled the construction end of their operation. Dwain would help facilitate new business, and Eddie James would draw up construction plans for their customers, and then begin putting up the buildings.

When they met in Dwane's office, the Kid laid out plans for his vision of a new CoCo Bed. On his property there was an ample supply of tall virgin timber which John Dempsey would have his crew cut and mill. The Kid told Dwain and Eddie James that he wanted a large colonial styled home for himself, Noah, Dennis, Jerry, and Yonie. He also wanted eight comfortable houses built to replace the old shotgun styled buildings that were occupied by the sharecroppers, in fact, lets build ten of these houses for an expanded crew. Eddie James DeRamus could always build more as needed. Finally he wanted a large building to be utilized as a school for children of the workers. He also wanted a boarding house type building for teachers at the school who wanted to live on the location.

Dwain, John Dempsey, and Eddie James were amazed at the size of this project, but assured the CoCo Bed Kid they would be able to handle it. John Dempsey said that he would arrange for extra crews and began harvesting the timber within a couple of days. Eddie James and Dwain said they would immediately start work on the building plans and could have something for the Kid within a week.

The men all stood and shook hands on this enormous deal. The Kid then got on Dolly and headed back to Mrs. Gallien's Boarding House. He was exhausted after the events of the morning. A lot had changed since breakfast this morning.

Chapter 29

Once he was fully rested, the CoCo Bed Kid called all of his people together for a meeting. Noah Johnson had not yet returned from his trip to Galveston. David Stamey was preparing for his trip to the Smoky Mountains to visit his family. The Kid told everyone present that he wanted them to stay at the Boarding House for a few weeks, especially Dennis and Yonie, to give their injuries time to heal properly. He told them that he now owned the CoCo Bed property, and had made arrangements to have new homes built for them all. Once he had gathered some supplies from the Masson Supply Store he told them, he planned to set up a camp on CoCo Bed.

Once he had all the supplies that he would need, the Kid mounted Dolly and began leading a pack horse loaded with supplies down the road to CoCo Bed.

When he arrived on CoCo Bed, the Kid stopped at each of the sharecropper shacks. He gave each a small bag of gold coins and told them to get all the things they needed to make themselves comfortable. He told them of his Coco Bed purchase and his plans to build each of them new houses. Many tears of joy and hugs were shared at every stop. He informed them to just sit back in comfort for a couple of months until it was time to harvest the cotton.

The Kid then rode down the road to where the remains of his burned home place was located. After finding a good spot near a stream that ran by where the old house had been, the Kid began to erect his tent and lay out his supplies.

Obviously he had the money to remain at Mrs. Gallien's Boarding House with the others, but he wanted some quiet time to reflect on events that would take place in the near future.

Once his camp was set up, the Kid walked over to the two graves of his loving Parents. Their lives had been horribly cut short by the Yankee soldiers, but his faith assured him they were definitely in a better place. The Kid hoped that they would be proud of him. He had done some things he was not proud of; however, with the good he had done for those less fortunate, he figured things perhaps evened out. The CoCo Bed Kid was a firm believer in Paying It Forward.

EPILOGUE

Six months had passed since we last heard from the Coco Bed Kid. It was a cool sunlit day as the Kid stood on the balcony of the beautiful colonial styled home that Dwain Johnson and his son Eddie James DeRamus had built. He gazed to his left and saw similar styled homes built for Noah Johnson, Dennis, Jerry, and Yonie. To his right stood twelve white structures that housed his work force. The Kid no longer wanted to refer to them as sharecroppers. In front he gazed at a beautiful two story school building, and next to it stood a magnificent structure that housed David Stamey, Doug Ireland, and Ginny VanSickle. The previous month they had opened their school doors, and everyone was thrilled by their professional work educating the children.

The cotton crop had been picked by his workers and sent to the gin in Cloutierville to be processed. The Kid had received an extremely generous price for his crop. He gave each family a nice bonus for their hard work.

The Sang Pour Sang Sawmill and Construction Company had done a remarkable job of harvesting the timber and had burned all the left over limbs to keep the pristine beauty of the tall virgin trees that remained. The large stand of virgin timber stood majestically swaying in the breeze and the abundant game ran wild. Dwain and Eddie James had done an excellent job of disposing the old lumber from the shotgun houses which stood where the newly built houses were. Enough space was allowed at each house for the occupants to grow gardens, as well as plants and flowers.

The wounds that had been inflicted on Dennis and Yonie had nicely healed, and both had become an important part of the Kid's new empire. He had also received a telegraph from Jean Laffitte and the Carr brothers. Noah had done a good job of delivering their gold, and Laffitte had made arrangements to send the Carrs theirs.

There was sadness to spoil the festivities of the day though. Dennis had received word that his old boss, as well as friend, John Murrell, had lost his life after contracting tuberculosis. He was buried near his home in the Smyrna First United Methodist Church Cemetery. Sadly, after he had been buried, parts of his body had been stolen as grave robbers dug him up. The CoCo Bed Kid and his old gang would certainly miss him.

As the Kid gazed from his balcony, there was gayety from below. There was long tables, heaped with barbecued beef and pork, vegetables, baked bread, and delicious cakes and other deserts, that had been prepared by the ladies who lived on CoCo Bed.

A small group of musicians played on a small stage set up to entertain the crowd. A young man named Marvin Kerry, a local musician and his friends, had kept the music going most of the morning.

Everyone was enjoying themselves. The CoCo Bed Kid smiled to himself as a thought ran through his mind.

Pay It Forward was indeed a Blessed concept.

david carr

Printed in the United States
By Bookmasters